Castle

POLICE

Chemist

Florist

Hospital

Post Office

This is Postman Pete. He loves
delivering letters and parcels to
everyone in Story Town – and he
loves surprises, too!

A catalogue record for this book is available from the British Library

Published by Ladybird Books Ltd
27 Wrights Lane London W8 5TZ
A Penguin Company

2 4 6 8 10 9 7 5 3 1

© LADYBIRD BOOKS LTD MMI

LADYBIRD and the device of a Ladybird are trademarks of Ladybird Books Ltd

Little Workmates

Postman Pete

by Ronne Randall
illustrated by Emma Dodd

Ladybird

Postman Pete
jumped out of bed.

"Hooray!" he said.
"It's my birthday!
I can't wait to
see how many
birthday cards
I get."

At the post office,
Postman Pete sorted the
mail and filled his sack.
But there were no cards
for him.

"Perhaps I'll get some
when I deliver the mail,"
he thought.

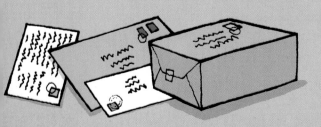

"Good morning, Florist Fern,"
said Postman Pete.

"I have some letters and
a parcel for
you today."

"It's my new flowerpot!"
said Fern. "Thank you,
Postman Pete!"
And with that she
went inside.

"No birthday
card?" thought
Postman Pete.
"Perhaps at my
next stop..."

PETE

"Good morning, PC Polly," said Postman Pete at the police station. "I have some letters and a postcard for you today!"

"It's my new flowerpot!" said Fern. "Thank you, Postman Pete!" And with that she went inside.

"No birthday card?" thought Postman Pete. "Perhaps at my next stop..."

"Good morning, PC Polly," said Postman Pete at the police station. "I have some letters and a postcard for you today!"

"It's from my friend Pippa in Peru!" said Polly. "Thank you, Postman Pete."

And with that she went back to her work.

"No birthday card?" thought Postman Pete with a sigh. "Perhaps at my next stop..."

"Good morning, Mr Baker!" said Pete. "I have three letters and a parcel for you today!"

"It's my new rolling pin!" said Mr Baker. "Thank you, Postman Pete!"

And with that he carried on with his work.

"No birthday card here, either," thought Postman Pete, feeling very glum.

The last two letters in Postman Pete's sack were for Fireman Fergus.

"I hope Fergus has a birthday card for me," he thought.

But Fireman Fergus had nothing for Postman Pete.

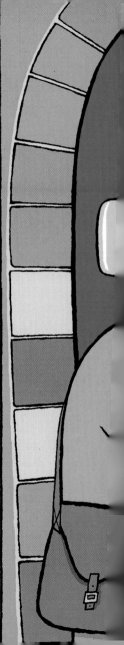

Postman Pete felt very sad.

"Everyone has forgotten my birthday," he thought as he walked home.

But when he got to his house...

"SURPRISE!"

Everyone was there –
with cards, and presents,
and a **big** birthday cake!
"Happy Birthday,
Postman Pete!"
they cheered.

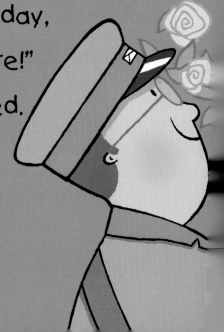

Postman Pete opened his presents and shared his cake with everyone.

"This is the best birthday I've ever had!" he said.